The **Cherry Blossom Tree**

A Grandfather Talks about Life and Death

For my grandchildren

The Cherry Blossom Tree

A Grandfather Talks about Life and Death

Jan Godfrey
Illustrated by Jane Cope

Augsburg
MINNEAPOLIS

It was Grandpa's birthday. Harriet and the cousins had come to his birthday party. Harriet had drawn a great many tiny kisses on her card for Grandpa.

"There's hundreds and thousands and millions of kisses all for you, because you're so old," said Harriet happily. "How old are you, Grandpa?"

"Very old," said Grandpa.

"I am five," said Harriet. "Will I be old soon?"

"Not just yet," said Grandpa, smiling.

Harriet smiled back and ate a very large slice of birthday cake.

One of Grandpa's presents was a shiny
new spade.
"I'll try it out right away," said Grandpa.
"I'll help," said Harriet.

They went to the wild part of the garden where the long grass and dandelions and apple trees grew.

Harriet blew on a dandelion. She stood watching the fluffy seeds floating into the blue sky.

"Where do the dandelion seeds go?" asked Harriet.

"Over the hills and far away," said Grandpa. "Then they fall into the earth, and next year they grow into new dandelions."

Harriet ran to the very end of the garden. Grandpa walked more slowly because he had stiff knees.

Every year on Grandpa's birthday, Harriet's favorite cherry tree was covered in pink blossoms.

But the cherry tree wasn't there!

"Where's it gone?" asked Harriet in surprise.

She stood on the stump. Branches of the cherry tree lay on the ground.

"It fell down," said Grandpa. "It was very, very old, and time for it to die."

Harriet held Grandpa's big hand tightly and they looked at the wild garden together.

"You're very, very old," she said anxiously. "Are you going to die?"

She remembered how much she'd cried when Smokey, her dog, had died.

She felt sad. She loved Grandpa very much.

"Please don't die, Grandpa," said Harriet.

"Everything that is born has to die sometime," said Grandpa. "And that makes us sad. But death is a new beginning, like waking up after a long sleep.

"God loves us so much and wants us to be together, even after our bodies have worn out."

"Everyone?" asked Harriet. "Everything?"

She thought about tiny ants, and wriggly worms, and huge elephants, and snakes, and snails, and tortoises.

"Everything is new and different where God is," said Grandpa. "We call it heaven. Anyone who loves God can go to be with him when they die."

"What's heaven like?" asked Harriet.

"I don't know," said Grandpa. "But imagine you're a new chick inside an eggshell. The world you see is all quite dark. Then one day you hatch into our big world and it's all bright and dazzly and different."

Harriet shut her eyes. She pretended she was a new chick hatching into Grandpa's sunny garden. When she opened her eyes the sun was dazzling.

The garden was beautiful!

"In heaven, we'll be different too," said
Grandpa. "But you'll know me, and I'll know
you. And we'll have new bodies that won't hurt
or creak or wear out or get tired or get old or
ill. Think of a caterpillar. One day it turns into a
dull brown chrysalis and then . . . "

"Then it's a beautiful, beautiful butterfly!"
said Harriet. She flew around the garden on
pretend butterfly wings.

"Do you remember those poppy seeds
last summer?" asked Grandpa. "They looked
like dust, but they'll grow into lovely red . . ."
"Poppies!" said Harriet.

Grandpa dug down into the earth with his shiny new spade.

"Look, there's a cherry pit!" said Harriet.

The cherry pit had split open and a little seedling was growing from it.

"That shoot has started to grow down there in the dark earth," said Grandpa.

"One day, after a long, long time, it will grow into a new cherry tree with blossoms and cherries. It won't look a bit like a pit then. Shall we plant it again?"

Harriet clapped her hands. She and Grandpa planted the little cherry pit together.

Harriet was glad that God made everything new and alive.

God made chicks hatch out of shells, and caterpillars turn into butterflies. God made dusty seeds grow into poppies, and cherry trees grow out of little pits.

She jumped up and blew another dandelion.

"Six o'clock!" said Grandpa, picking up the shiny new spade. "Time to go indoors. There's another day tomorrow."

They went back to the house together.

The cousins were looking at old photographs. One of them was of Grandpa when he was a little boy. He did look different!

"Where have you been?" asked the cousins.

"Planting a new cherry tree," said Harriet.

"With my new shiny spade," said Grandpa.

And Grandpa and Harriet smiled at each other as they thought about God's new beginnings, and the cherry tree's wonderful secret.

THE CHERRY BLOSSOM TREE
A Grandfather Talks about Life and Death

First North American edition published 1996 by Augsburg Fortress, Minneapolis.
First published by Tamarind Books in London, England.

ISBN 0-8066-2843-X   LCCN 95-079332

Manufactured in Singapore.   AF 9-2843

00   99   98   97   96   1   2   3   4   5   6   7   8   9   10